U0092511

The Crescent Moon

新月集

泰戈爾　著

糜文開、糜榴麗　譯

國家圖書館出版品預行編目資料

新月集 / 泰戈爾著；糜文開,糜榴麗譯. －－初版一刷. －－
臺北市：三民，2018
　　面；　公分. －－(世界文學)
　　ISBN 978－957－14－6404－6　(平裝)

867.51　　　　　　　　　　　　　　　　　107005426

© 　新 月 集

著 作 人	泰戈爾
譯　　者	糜文開　糜榴麗
插畫設計	蔡瓅崴

發 行 人	劉振強
著作財產權人	三民書局股份有限公司
發 行 所	三民書局股份有限公司
	地址　臺北市復興北路386號
	電話　(02)25006600
	郵撥帳號　0009998－5
門 市 部	(復北店)臺北市復興北路386號
	(重南店)臺北市重慶南路一段61號

| 出版日期 | 初版一刷　2018年9月 |
| 編　　號 | S 870140 |

行政院新聞局登記證局版臺業字第○二○○號

有著作權‧不准侵害

ISBN　978－957－14－6404－6　　(平裝)

http://www.sanmin.com.tw　三民網路書店

泰戈爾在臺灣的代言人：糜文開

　　印度，有點熟悉又遙遠神祕的國度。古遠的天竺故事和印度歌舞人人皆有印象，但印度現代的歷史和文學卻又似乎相當陌生。泰戈爾可能是大家最容易想到的現代印度作家了：身為亞洲首位獲得諾貝爾文學獎的詩人，泰戈爾在二十世紀前半的中國名聲響亮，不但曾親訪中國，與徐志摩、林徽因的交往讓人津津樂道，梁啟超也為他取了個中文名字「竺震旦」。鄭振鐸在 1922 年譯出了他的《飛鳥集》，更是傳頌一時。

　　但在戰後的臺灣，五四詩人已遠，《飛鳥集》因鄭振鐸「附匪」而名列禁書書單，泰戈爾的名聲仍得以維持不墜，必須歸功於糜文開。臺灣市面上雖能見到鄭振鐸的《飛鳥集》，例如江南、輔新、漢風等出版社的版本，但都不署譯者名字，且書名一律都改為《漂鳥集》，也是因為糜文開的緣故。至今兩岸新譯本不絕，但無論譯者是誰，中國至今仍以《飛鳥集》為主流，臺灣還是繼續稱為《漂鳥集》，兩岸各有定譯，也是頗為有趣的現象。

糜文開 (1908–1983) 是江蘇無錫人，中華民國外交官，1940 年代長駐印度，也在印度國際大學哲學系進修，與印度淵源甚深。1948 年，他在印度大使館長夏無事，和同事容寶琛兩人偶然發現鄭振鐸的《飛鳥集》不全，且誤譯處不少，於是重譯此書，改書名為《漂鳥集》，理由是「漂鳥」比「飛鳥」更符合印度崇尚雲遊漂泊修行者的意象。序中說當初翻譯此詩集純為「消夏」，初無出版之計畫，他比較急於出版的是 1948 年上半年已經譯完的《奈都夫人詩全集》。為了這本詩集，他不但跟作者奈都夫人合照，夫人也寫了幾句給中文讀者的話，又請了駐印度大使羅家倫寫序，一切準備妥當，寄去上海商務準備出版。誰知 1949 年時局大亂，上海商務説無法出版了，糜文開羈留香港，只好自己開起出版社來。出版社叫做「印度研究社」，專出糜文開和女兒糜榴麗兩人譯作。原本計畫出五本書，第五本即《泰戈爾詩總集》，包含已譯完的《漂鳥集》和《新月集》，不過後來只出了前四種，《泰戈爾詩總集》並未在香港出版。

糜文開 1953 年來到臺灣，繼續外交官生涯，也在大學教印度文學。1955 年，應朋友要求，在香港大學生活月刊連載早已譯出的《漂鳥集》，許多讀者為之驚豔，三民書局遂在 1956 年出版《漂鳥集》單行本。此後「漂鳥」成為臺灣的定譯，儘管臺灣還有周策縱在美國譯的《失群的鳥》和羅青的《單飛的鳥》，但都無法取代《漂鳥集》在讀者心中的地

位。糜文開與糜榴麗父女合譯的《新月集》也繼《漂
鳥集》後出版。糜文開又陸續與夫人裴溥言合譯其
他五冊泰戈爾詩集，1958 年出齊七冊。此時距離他
在新德里消夏時翻譯《漂鳥集》已有十年，他自己
漂泊港臺，歷經喪偶與新婚，境遇憂喜交織，恍若
隔世，也見證了戰後文人流離遷徙的動亂時光。

　　《漂鳥集》和《新月集》風格完全不同。《漂鳥
集》是精緻玲瓏的浮光掠影，短短一兩句人生哲理
沁人心脾，的確足以「消夏」；《新月集》卻是童趣
十足，親子情深之作，幾首敘事詩有情有景，難以
忘懷。每一本譯作都與譯者的生命歷程交織而成，
今天重看糜文開翻譯的泰戈爾詩作，似乎還能感受
到 1948 年印度的那一個漫漫長夏呢！

師大翻譯研究所教授　賴慈芸

二〇一八年三月

序

「瓶花妥帖爐煙定，覓我童心十六年。」龔定
盦這兩句詩的意境，確是數千年中國詩史所罕有，
我們這個民族是以敬老尚齒聞於世界的。我們是以
「齒」、「爵」、「德」為三達德，以「年高德劭」、
「槁項黃馘」為尊敬的對象；便是對於少年人，我
們也希望他「老成」，對於兒童，則竟要鼓勵他「弱
不好弄」。「童心」在人是嘲笑的批評，在文學上則
從來搜不出這麼個辭彙。勉強說來，唯「稚氣」、「天
真」有依稀近似處，但誰都知道前者是我們文學上
不可容忍的缺點，後者與「童心」還有莫大距離。

據說動物的記憶力是極薄弱的，動物而愈下等，
則記憶亦愈劣。蝴蝶雖是美麗生物，但牠也只算是
下等生物。牠生長的過程又遠比人類來得繁複。人
一出母胎，便一路生長上去，而蝴蝶則要經過毛蟲、

蛹、成蟲三個階段。這三個階段使蝴蝶生命截然分
而為三，不相連續。我敢同你打賭：即使蝴蝶中間
有記憶力最強的，當牠飛舞花叢，栩然自得之際，
決記不起牠自己過去做毛蟲和蛹時的生活。不但全
部記不起，模糊恍惚的影子都不會有。

所以，蝴蝶儘管文彩輝煌得可愛，牠始終只是
個可憐的昆蟲！

但是，我又敢同你打賭：你是萬物之靈的人類，
你自嬰孩發展而為成人，自成人成熟而為中年老年。
成人以下的三個階段，你也許記憶得相當清楚，那
嬰孩的階段，模糊恍惚的影子也許有——這確是我
們萬物之靈勝於昆蟲之處——可是你能把那些記
憶，淋漓盡致一絲不走地表達出來，形容出來嗎？
你能縮回你的生命，扭轉你的想像，倒流你無憂的
歲月，恢復你天真爛漫的心情，以孩童的眼睛來觀
察這繽紛多彩的世界，以孩童的耳朵來聽這萬籟共
鳴的聲音，以孩童的口吻來說出你的驚奇、喜悅、

恐懼、興奮、愛好嗎？我知道你一定會對我連連搖手，我辦不到，辦不到。尼閣德睦對耶穌說：人不能重入母腹而為嬰兒，你要我做的事，雖不至於像重入母腹之難，卻也差不多了。誰又能記得那毫無意義孩童時代的一切呢？即使記得，有什麼適當的辭彙、語法來寫述出來呢？

對呀，這件事果然不很容易，是以西洋童話家雖彬彬輩出，也只有安徒生、格林兄弟等幾個人稱為翹楚。在我們中國則點起亮亮的燈籠，打起明晃晃的火把找不出一個半個。為了這緣故，我們的兒童時代從來沒聽見過什麼國王、公主、仙女、巨人；我們的文學，也從來沒有什麼駕著駟馬金車馳騁天空的阿波羅，執著雙蛇棒帶領亡靈沿著銀河走入地府的赫梅士。因之我們也缺乏沉博絕麗，恢奇俊偉，像荷馬、魏琪爾所作的詩篇。我們民族的腦筋，自幼便被強揉在修齊治平的模子裡，鑄成了一副死板的型式。我們的文學是蒼白的、萎黃的、枯槁的、矯揉造作的、千篇一律程式化的，缺乏真純的趣味和青春的活力，也缺乏偉大的想像，和天馬行空、不受羈勒的創造天才。

因此，即以定盦先生而論，他也許能在瓶花弄影，爐煙裊裊的境界裡，重新覓得他那十六年前早經消逝的童心，但我們卻只能在他的詩詞中，體認他少年綺怨的幽咽，壯歲意氣的飛揚，暮年逃空的寂寞，表現童心的文字卻一個字也看不見。我想定盦先生或者要答覆我們道：這和隱士的山中白雲一樣，「只可自怡悅，不堪持贈君。」當然，這只是他解嘲的話，寫不出才是真實的形況。

印度這個國家民族的歷史也許比我們還古老得多，但他們雖也尊敬老人，卻並不希望少年老成，鼓勵兒童弱不好弄；反之，他們從古以來，便有無數禽獸擬人的童話，寫入典重的文字，竄入莊嚴的經典。他們又有兩部著名的史詩，一部是《羅摩耶那》，一部是《摩訶婆羅多》。印度人自兒童時代便讀起，一

直讀到頭童齒豁尚有餘味 。 印度全民族不分貧富貴
賤，不問男女老幼，沒有不知這兩部史詩的事跡和詩
中英雄之作為的。這在兒童文學的寫作上，印度人所
憑藉者比我們當然要豐富千百倍了 。 詩哲泰戈爾的
《新月集》則更是印度這類文學裡提煉出來的精
華，也可說是世界絕無僅有的一部傑作。他寫這部詩
集對於印度的文學遺產，當然有所借重，但他若沒有
那五個婉孌可愛的小天使和他那溫柔嫻淑的夫
人，朝夕周旋，我想他還是寫不出這類好詩來的。你
看《新月集》這部詩，泰戈爾真的走回了他自己的孩
童時代，以純粹兒童的官感、心靈來認識這世界，歌
唱這世界，讚頌這世界。現在請你且讀以下的詩句：

　　母親，我真正相信花兒是到地下上學去的。

　　他們把門關著讀書，若是他們要未到時間就
出來玩耍，他們的教師就要叫他們立壁角的。

　　當雨季到來，他們就放假了。

森林的枝條相擊，在野風中葉子發沙沙聲，雷雲們拍著他們巨大的手，花朵孩童們就衝出來了，穿著粉紅、鵝黃與雪白服裝。（〈花校〉）

巷裡黑暗而寂寞，街燈站在那裡像一個巨人，他的頭上有一隻紅眼睛。（〈職業〉）

這完全是孩童的癡話，然而卻是充滿著大人們永遠自愧不如的想像力的癡話。

我個人所喜愛的是〈孩兒之歌〉、〈睡眠的偷竊者〉、〈誹謗〉、〈雲與浪〉、〈香伯花〉、〈商人〉、〈英雄〉那幾首，不過說句老實話，《新月集》的四十首詩內容雖各殊，卻有同等的價值。泰戈爾在這閃著琥珀色奇光的兒童王國裡設了一席盛宴，歡迎任何人的參加。惟一條件是要你把那件滿沾「世途經歷」之灰塵的長袍，脫卸在這王國的大門之外，帶著一顆赤裸的「童心」進去！

蘇雪林

新月集 The Crescent Moon 目次

新月集

The
Crescent
Moon

家

我獨自在田野的路上緩步前進,落日似守財奴般收藏他最後的黃金。

那日光深深下沉,沉入黑暗之中,那孤寂的大地靜悄悄地躺著,地上的收穫已經刈割掉。

驀地裡一個小孩的尖銳聲音衝向天空。他橫亙這冥漠的黑暗,放出他歌聲的波痕來劃破這黃昏的靜默。

他的農舍之家在這光禿土地盡頭處的蔗田那一邊,隱藏在香蕉和纖長檳榔棕,椰子與墨綠色榴槤樹的重重濃蔭中。

在我寂寞的途中,我在星光下停留了一會,看見展開在我面前那黑越越的大地用兩臂環抱著無數的家,配備著搖籃和床,母親的心與黃昏的燈,還有幼小的生靈們因歡樂而歡樂,可是並不知道這對於世界的價值啊。

THE HOME

I paced alone on the road across the field while the sunset was hiding its last gold like a miser.

The daylight sank deeper and deeper into the darkness, and the widowed land, whose harvest had been reaped, lay silent.

Suddenly a boy's shrill voice rose into the sky. He traversed the dark unseen, leaving the track of his song across the hush of the evening.

His village home lay there at the end of the waste land, beyond the sugar-cane field, hidden among the shadows of the banana and the slender areca palm, the cocoa-nut and the dark green jack-fruit trees.

I stopped for a moment in my lonely way under the starlight, and saw spread before me the darkened earth surrounding with her arms countless homes furnished with cradles and beds, mothers' hearts and evening lamps, and young lives glad with a gladness that knows nothing of its value for the world.

海　邊

在這無垠世界的海邊，孩子們相會。

這遼闊的天宇靜止在上空，這流動的水波喧噪著。

在這無垠世界的海邊，孩子們相會，叫著，跳著。

他們用沙造他們的房屋，他們用空的貝殼玩著。用枯葉織成他們的船，一隻隻含笑地浮到大海裡去。在這世界的海灘上，孩子們自有他們的玩意兒。

他們不懂得怎樣游泳，他們不懂得怎樣撒網。採珠者潛水摸珠，商人在船上航行，可是孩子們把卵石聚集起來又撒開去。他們不搜尋寶藏，他們不懂得怎樣去撒網。

海水大笑著掀起波濤，蒼白閃耀著海灘的笑容。兇險的浪濤對孩子們唱著無意義的歌曲，就像一個母親正在搖著她嬰孩的搖籃。大海與孩子們一起玩著，蒼白閃耀著海灘的笑容。

ON THE SEASHORE

On the seashore of endless worlds children meet.
The infinite sky is motionless overhead and the
restless water is boisterous. On the seashore of endless
worlds the children meet with shouts and dances.

∞≍≍∞

They build their houses with sand, and they play with
empty shells. With withered leaves they weave their
boats and smilingly float them on the vast deep.
Children have their play on the seashore of worlds.

∞≍≍∞

They know not how to swim, they know not how to
cast nets. Pearl-fishers dive for pearls, merchants sail
in their ships, while children gather pebbles and
scatter them again. They seek not for hidden treasures,
they know not how to cast nets.

∞≍≍∞

The sea surges up with laughter, and pale gleams the
smile of the sea-beach. Death-dealing waves sing
meaningless ballads to the children, even like a mother
while rocking her baby's cradle. The sea plays with
children, and pale gleams the smile of the sea-beach.

∞≍≍∞

在無垠世界的海邊孩子們相會。暴風雨遨遊在無徑
的天空，船隻破裂在無軌可循的水中。死神已出來
而孩子們在玩耍。在無垠世界的海邊是孩子們的偉
大相會。

On the seashore of endless worlds children meet.
Tempest roams in the pathless sky, ships are wrecked
in the trackless water, death is abroad and children
play. On the seashore of endless worlds is the great
meeting of children.

泉　源

睡眠撲翅飛息在孩兒的眼睛上──是否有人知道這睡眠來自何處？是的，有一個傳聞說，睡眠居住在森林濃蔭中的神仙莊。那裡，螢火蟲放著朦朧的微光；那裡，懸垂著兩個迷人的羞澀花蕾。睡眠就從那裡飛來吻著孩兒的眼睛。

微笑閃動在孩兒的嘴唇上，當他睡眠的時候──是否有人知道這微笑誕生在何處？是的，有一個傳聞說，一彎新月的初生之淡光碰觸著消散的秋雲之邊緣。那裡，微笑最初出生於一個露洗清晨的夢中──微笑閃動在孩兒的嘴唇上，當他睡眠的時候。

芬芳柔嫩的新鮮氣開放在孩兒的四肢上──是否有人知道這早先藏匿在何處？是的，當母親還是一個少女，它便充滿在她的心裡，在愛的關注與靜穆之神祕中──這芬芳柔嫩的新鮮氣已在孩兒的四肢上開放。

THE SOURCE

The sleep that flits on baby's eyes — does anybody know from where it comes? Yes, there is a rumour that it has its dwelling where, in the fairy village among shadows of the forest dimly lit with glow-worms, there hang two shy buds of enchantment. From there it comes to kiss baby's eyes.

The smile that flickers on baby's lips when he sleeps— does anybody know where it was born? Yes, there is a rumour that a young pale beam of a crescent moon touched the edge of a vanishing autumn cloud, and there the smile was first born in the dream of a dew-washed morning — the smile that flickers on baby's lips when he sleeps.

The sweet, soft freshness that blooms on baby's limbs— does anybody know where it was hidden so long? Yes, when the mother was a young girl it lay pervading her heart in tender and silent mystery of love — the sweet, soft freshness that has bloomed on baby's limbs.

孩兒之歌

假使孩兒要想這樣，他能即刻鼓翼飛向天堂。
這不是無故的，他沒有離開我們。
因為他連看不見母親也永遠不能忍受，孩兒愛把他
的小頭放在母親的胸懷。

❈❈❈

孩兒知道各種的智慧之辭，雖然世上很少人能了解
那些意思。
這不是無故的，他常不言不語。
他唯一的願望是從母親的唇邊來學習母親的說話，
這是他為什麼看來這樣渾噩。

❈❈❈

孩兒有大堆的金銀和珍珠，他卻似乞丐的模樣蒞臨
這世界。
這不是無故的，他要如此扮飾。
他要求母親的愛之珍藏，而這可愛的赤裸小乞是冒
充著全然無助。

❈❈❈

BABY'S WAY

If baby only wanted to, he could fly up to heaven this moment.

It is not for nothing that he does not leave us.

He loves to rest his head on mother's bosom, and cannot ever bear to lose sight of her.

Baby knows all manner of wise words, though few on earth can understand their meaning.

It is not for nothing that he never wants to speak.

The one thing he wants is to learn mother's words from mother's lips. That is why he looks so innocent.

Baby had a heap of gold and pearls, yet he came like a beggar on to this earth.

It is not for nothing he came in such a disguise.

This dear little naked mendicant pretends to be utterly helpless, so that he may beg for mother's wealth of love.

孩兒在纖細的新月之鄉沒有什麼約束。

這不是無故的，他放棄了自由。

他知道在母親的心之角裡有無窮的歡樂之所，撫抱
在她親愛的兩臂之中，是遠比自由為甜蜜。

———————◇◇◇———————

孩兒從來不知啼哭，他住在一個完全幸福的境邑。

這不是無故的，他選擇流淚。

雖然他可愛面龐上的微笑吸引著母親渴望的心向
他，但在小小的困苦上哭幾聲卻織著愛和憐的雙結。

Baby was so free from every tie in the land of the tiny crescent moon.

It was not for nothing he gave up his freedom.

He knows that there is room for endless joy in mother's little corner of a heart, and it is sweeter far than liberty to be caught and pressed in her dear arms.

Baby never knew how to cry. He dwelt in the land of perfect bliss.

It is not for nothing he has chosen to shed tears.

Though with the smile of his dear face he draws mother's yearning heart to him, yet his little cries over tiny troubles weave the double bond of pity and love.

生命的小蕾

啊，我的小孩，是誰染色那件小衣服，把你的美麗
的四肢遮上那小小的紅衣？

你早晨到院子裡來玩，你跑路時搖擺著，顛躓著。

但是，我的孩子，是誰染色那件小衣服？

我的生命的小蕾，什麼使你歡笑？

母親站在門階上對你微笑。

她拍著手，她的鐲子就叮叮璫璫，你手裡拿著竹竿
像一個細小的牧夫跳著舞。

但是，我的生命的小蕾，什麼使你歡笑？

哦，小乞，你乞求什麼，用你的雙手纏在母親的頸
項上？

哦，貪多的心，是不是要我把世界像一個果子一樣
從天上摘下來放在你紅潤的小手掌中？

哦，小乞，你乞求什麼？

THE UNHEEDED PAGEANT

Ah, who was it coloured that little frock, my child,
and covered your sweet limbs with that little red tunic?
You have come out in the morning to play in the
courtyard, tottering and tumbling as you run.
But who was it coloured that little frock, my child?

What is it makes you laugh, my little life-bud?
Mother smiles at you standing on the threshold.
She claps her hands and her bracelets jingle, and you
dance with your bamboo stick in your hand like a tiny
little shepherd.
But what is it makes you laugh, my little life-bud?

O beggar, what do you beg for, clinging to your
mother's neck with both your hands?
O greedy heart, shall I pluck the world like a fruit
from the sky to place it on your little rosy palm?
O beggar, what are you begging for?

風歡快地帶走你的踝鈴的玎玲聲。

太陽笑著看你的梳洗。

你在母親懷中睡眠時天空守著你,而清晨小心翼翼
地到你床邊來吻你眼睛。

風歡快地帶走你的踝鈴的玎玲聲。

那夢之主的仙女穿過薄暮的天空向你飛來。

在母親的心中,世界母親留著她的地位在你旁邊。

他,對星星奏音樂的人,拿著他的笛站在你窗下。

那是夢之主的仙女穿過薄暮的天空向你飛來。

The wind carries away in glee the tinkling of your anklet bells.

The sun smiles and watches your toilet.

The sky watches over you when you sleep in your mother's arms, and the morning comes tiptoe to your bed and kisses your eyes.

The wind carries away in glee the tinkling of your anklet bells.

><><><

The fairy mistress of dreams is coming towards you, flying through the twilight sky.

The world-mother keeps her seat by you in your mother's heart.

He who plays his music to the stars is standing at your window with his flute.

And the fairy mistress of dreams is coming towards you, flying through the twilight sky.

睡眠的偷竊者

誰從孩兒的眼睛偷竊了睡眠？我一定要知道。

母親把水瓶抱在她腰部到附近的村莊去汲水。

正午時候小孩們的玩耍時間已過；池子裡的鴨子群
也靜默了。

牧童躺在榕樹的蔭影下瞌睡。

白鶴莊嚴而沉默地站立在檬果林畔的水澤中。

就在這時候，睡眠的偷竊者到來，乘機從孩兒的眼
睛攫取了睡眠飛走。

當母親回來，她發現孩兒用四肢在屋裡遊歷。

SLEEP-STEALER

Who stole sleep from baby's eyes? I must know.

Clasping her pitcher to her waist mother went to fetch water from the village near by.

It was noon. The children's playtime was over; the ducks in the pond were silent.

The shepherd boy lay asleep under the shadow of the *banyan* tree.

The crane stood grave and still in the swamp near the mango grove.

In the meanwhile the Sleep-stealer came and, snatching sleep from baby's eyes, flew away.

When mother came back she found baby travelling the room over on all fours.

⋘⋙

誰從我們孩兒的眼睛偷竊了睡眠？我一定要知道，
我一定找到她把她鎖起來。

我一定經過那些圓石和怒石，在流出一條小溪的地
方去探看那暗洞。

我一定到鈸古拉叢的朦朧蔭影去覓尋，那裡，有鴿
子在一隅和鳴，仙人的踝鈴在星夜的靜寂中玎璫。

在黃昏，我將窺視那竹林的低語之靜寂，那裡螢火
蟲揮霍牠們的光，我將對我遇到的每一樣生物詢問：
「那一個能告訴我睡眠的偷竊者住在那裡？」

Who stole sleep from our baby's eyes? I must know. I must find her and chain her up.

I must look into that dark cave, where, through boulders and scowling stones, trickles a tiny stream.

I must search in the drowsy shade of the *bakula* grove, where pigeons coo in their corner, and fairies' anklets tinkle in the stillness of starry nights.

In the evening I will peep into the whispering silence of the bamboo forest, where fireflies squander their light, and will ask every creature I meet, "Can anybody tell me where the Sleep-stealer lives?"

誰從孩兒的眼睛偷竊了睡眠？我一定要知道。

只要我能捉住她，難道我不給她一個好教訓！

我將搜查她的巢穴，查看所有她藏放她偷來的睡眠的地方。

我要把它全部搶著帶回來。

我要把她的兩隻翅膀牢牢地縛住，把她放在河濱。

於是讓她用蘆葦做釣魚的玩兒，在燈心草與蓮花之間。

當傍晚市集時間已過，村童們坐在他們母親的膝上。

於是夜鳥們將嘲弄她，向她聒耳朵：

「你現在要偷誰的睡眠？」

Who stole sleep from baby's eyes? I must know.

Shouldn't I give her a good lesson if I could only catch her!

I would raid her nest and see where she hoards all her stolen sleep.

I would plunder it all, and carry it home.

I would bind her two wings securely, set her on the bank of the river, and then let her play at fishing with a reed among the rushes and water-lilies.

When the marketing is over in the evening, and the village children sit in their mothers' laps, then the night birds will mockingly din her ears with:

"Whose sleep will you steal now?"

來　源

「我從那裡來的，你在那裡拾到我？」孩子問他的母親。

她半笑半啼地回答，緊抱著孩子在她的懷抱裡，——

「我的寶貝，你是藏在我心裡的願望。

你在我童年玩弄的洋娃娃中；當每晨我做我神祇的塑像；我就做你又毀你。

你同我們的家神一起被尊為神，在他的崇拜中我就崇拜你。

在所有我的希望裡，我的愛裡，在我生命中，在我母親的生命中你居住著。

在那管理我們家的不死『精神』的懷抱裡你已被養育著很久。

在少女時代我的心開放花瓣時你就像芳香在上面翱翔。

你的柔和之甜蜜在我年輕的四肢上開花，像天上的曙光在旭日升起前。

天的第一個寶貝，同晨光學生，你漂下世界生命的河流來，最後你纏在我心上了。

當我看著你的臉，叫我不可思議；屬於全體的你，現在變做我的了。

因怕失去你的緣故，緊抱你在我懷抱裡。什麼魔術把世界的寶物網羅在我纖弱的雙臂中？」

THE BEGINNING

"Where have I come from, where did you pick me up?" the baby asked its mother.

She answered half crying, half laughing, and clasping the baby to her breast,—

"You were hidden in my heart as its desire, my darling.

You were in the dolls of my childhood's games; and when with clay I made the image of my god every morning, I made and unmade you then.

You were enshrined with our household deity, in his worship I worshipped you.

In all my hopes and my loves, in my life, in the life of my mother you have lived.

In the lap of the deathless Spirit who rules our home you have been nursed for ages.

When in girlhood my heart was opening its petals, you hovered as a fragrance about it.

Your tender softness bloomed in my youthful limbs, like a glow in the sky before the sunrise.

Heaven's first darling, twin-born with the morning light, you have floated down the stream of the world's life, and at last you have stranded on my heart.

As I gaze on your face, mystery overwhelms me; you who belong to all have become mine.

For fear of losing you I hold you tight to my breast. What magic has snared the world's treasure in these slender arms of mine?"

孩子的世界

我願我能獲得我孩子自己世界之中心的靜寂一角。

我知道那裡有星星對他講話，那裡有天空俯身下來到他臉上來用痴雲和虹霓娛樂他。

那些假裝是不會說話的，看是永不能動彈的，都爬到他的窗前來講故事，或帶來淺碟裡面裝滿了光亮的玩具。

我願我能旅行於經過孩子之心的路上，能解脫一切的束縛；

那裡使者無故出使奔跑於無來歷國王的國土間；

那裡「理性」用自己的定律做風箏來放，「真理」使「事實」從桎梏中得到自由。

BABY'S WORLD

I wish I could take a quiet corner in the heart of my baby's very own world.

I know it has stars that talk to him, and a sky that stoops down to his face to amuse him with its silly clouds and rainbows.

Those who make believe to be dumb, and look as if they never could move, come creeping to his window with their stories and with trays crowded with bright toys.

I wish I could travel by the road that crosses baby's mind, and out beyond all bounds;

Where messengers run errands for no cause between the kingdoms of kings of no history;

Where Reason makes kites of her laws and flies them, and Truth sets Fact free from its fetters.

領　悟

當我帶給你彩色的玩具，我的孩子，我明白為什麼
有這樣顏色的變幻在雲霞上，在水面上。為什麼花
要染著色彩——當我把彩色的玩具給你，我的孩子。
當我唱著歌使你跳舞，我才真正知道為什麼樹葉裡
有音樂，為什麼浪濤傳出合唱曲到靜聽之大地的心
裡去——當我唱著歌使你跳舞的時候。
當我帶糖果給你貪得的手，我知道為什麼花之杯中
有蜜，為什麼水果暗地裡飽含著甜漿——當我帶糖
果給你貪得的手的時候。
當我吻著你臉使你微笑，我的寶貝，我確實明白什
麼是晨光裡從天上瀉下來的喜悅，什麼是夏天的涼
風帶給我身體的愉快——當我吻你使你微笑的時
候。

WHEN AND WHY

When I bring you coloured toys, my child, I understand why there is such a play of colours on clouds, on water, and why flowers are painted in tints — when I give coloured toys to you, my child.

When I sing to make you dance, I truly know why there is music in leaves, and why waves send their chorus of voices to the heart of the listening earth — when I sing to make you dance.

When I bring sweet things to your greedy hands, I know why there is honey in the cup of the flower, and why fruits are secretly filled with sweet juice — when I bring sweet things to your greedy hands.

When I kiss your face to make you smile, my darling, I surely understand what pleasure streams from the sky in morning light, and what delight the summer breeze brings to my body — when I kiss you to make you smile.

誹　謗

我的孩子，為什麼你眼睛裡流著淚？

他們是多麼討厭，無緣無故地常常罵著你？

你寫字時用墨水染汙你的臉與手——為這事他們叫你骯髒？

呸！他們敢把那團團的明月叫做骯髒嗎，因為他把自己的臉塗上墨水？

～～～～～

一點點小事情他們就責難你，我的孩子。他們準備無故來挑剔。

遊玩時你把衣服撕破——為這事他們就說你不整潔？

呸！他們把一個從破爛的雲中微笑的秋晨叫做什麼呢？

～～～～～

我的孩子，別理他們對你說的話。

他們把你的過失寫得一大堆。

人人知道你是愛糖果的——就為這事他們叫你貪嘴嗎？

呸！那麼他們把我們愛你的人叫做什麼？

DEFAMATION

Why are those tears in your eyes, my child?
How horrid of them to be always scolding you for nothing?
You have stained your fingers and face with ink while writing — is that why they call you dirty?
O, fie! Would they dare to call the full moon dirty because it has smudged its face with ink?

For every little trifle they blame you, my child. They are ready to find fault for nothing.
You tore your clothes while playing — is that why they call you untidy?
O, fie! What would they call an autumn morning that smiles through its ragged clouds?

Take no heed of what they say to you, my child.
They make a long list of your misdeeds.
Everybody knows how you love sweet things — is that why they call you greedy?
O, fie! What then would they call us who love you?

裁　判

說他怎麼樣，隨便你，但我知道我的孩子的弱點。

不是因為他好我才愛他，只因為他是我的小孩。

你只試著衡量他的功和過孰多，你怎會知道他是多麼令人可愛？

當我不得不處罰他時，他格外成為我自己的一部分了。

當我使他流淚時，我的心也和他一同哭泣。

我自有權利去責罵和處罰，因為他只可由愛他的人來懲誡他。

THE JUDGE

Say of him what you please, but I know my child's failings.

I do not love him because he is good, but because he is my little child.

How should you know how dear he can be when you try to weigh his merits against his faults?

When I must punish him he becomes all the more a part of my being.

When I cause his tears to come my heart weeps with him.

I alone have a right to blame and punish, for he only may chastise who loves.

玩 具

孩子，你是多麼快活，你坐在塵埃中，整個早晨在
玩那折斷的小樹枝。

我笑你玩那小小的一細根折斷的樹枝。

我忙著我的計數，一點鐘，一點鐘的加著數目字。

或者，你瞥見我，你想，「這是多麼乏味的一種遊戲
來敗壞了你的早晨！」

孩子，我已忘記了專心致志於棒頭與泥餅的藝術。

我找出昂貴的玩具來，集合著一大批的金和銀。

你找到隨便什麼，你創造你的樂意的遊戲，我既浪
費我的時間，又浪費我的精力，去找我永無獲得的
東西。

在我易碎的獨木舟中，我努力渡越那願望之海，而
忘了我也是在玩著遊戲。

PLAYTHINGS

Child, how happy you are sitting in the dust, playing with a broken twig all the morning.

I smile at your play with that little bit of a broken twig.

I am busy with my accounts, adding up figures by the hour.

Perhaps you glance at me and think, "What a stupid game to spoil your morning with!"

Child, I have forgotten the art of being absorbed in sticks and mud-pies.

I seek out costly playthings, and gather lumps of gold and silver.

With whatever you find you create your glad games, I spend both my time and my strength over things I never can obtain.

In my frail canoe I struggle to cross the sea of desire, and forget that I too am playing a game.

天文家

我只說:「當黃昏時候那團團的月兒纏結在那棵『喀唐』樹的枝枒間,沒有人能捉住牠嗎?」

可是大大(哥哥)笑我說:「因因,你是我所知道的頂蠢的小孩。這月兒總是離我們很遠的,怎麼能夠有人捉住牠?」

我說:「大大,你是多麼笨啊!當母親向她的窗子外面探望,對我們下面的遊戲微笑著,你能說她很遠嗎?」

大大還是說:「你是一個小愚人!但是,因因,你那裡能夠找到一面大網可以用來捉月亮呢?」

我說:「當然,你能夠用手捉的。」

可是大大笑著說:「你是我所知道的頂蠢的小孩。如果天靠近來,你會看見月兒是怎樣大的。」

我說:「大大,他們在學校裡教你什麼胡說怪道!當母親俯身下來吻我們的時候,是不是她的臉看來很大?」

可是大大還是說:「你是一個小愚人。」

THE ASTRONOMER

I only said, "When in the evening the round full moon gets entangled among the branches of that *Kadam* tree, couldn't somebody catch it?"

But dādā laughed at me and said, "Baby, you are the silliest child I have ever known. The moon is ever so far from us, how could anybody catch it?"

I said, "Dādā how foolish you are! When mother looks out of her window and smiles down at us playing, would you call her far away?"

Still dādā said, "You are a stupid child! But, baby, where could you find a net big enough to catch the moon with?"

I said, "Surely you could catch it with your hands."

But dādā laughed and said, "You are the silliest child I have known. If it came nearer, you would see how big the moon is."

I said, "Dādā, what nonsense they teach at your school! When mother bends her face down to kiss us does her face look very big?"

But still dādā says, "You are a stupid child."

雲與浪

媽媽，那些住在雲中的人民對我喊著——
「我們遊玩，從我們醒來直到一日完了。
我們同金色的黎明玩，同銀色的月兒玩。」
我問：「不過我怎麼能到你們那邊來？」
他們回答：「到大地的邊緣那裡，舉起你的雙手向著
天空，你就會被帶上雲中來。」
「我的母親在家裡等待我回去，」我說：「我怎能離
她而到你們那邊來呢？」
於是他們笑笑飄去了。
但我知道比那更好的遊戲，媽媽。
我將是雲而你是月。
我將用兩手來遮蔽你，而我們的屋頂便變成青天。

CLOUDS AND WAVES

Mother, the folk who live up in the clouds call out to me—
"We play from the time we wake till the day ends.
We play with the golden dawn, we play with the silver moon."
I ask, "But, how am I to get up to you?"
They answer, "Come to the edge of the earth, lift up your hands to the sky, and you will be taken up into the clouds."
"My mother is waiting for me at home," I say. "How can I leave her and come?"
Then they smile and float away.
But I know a nicer game than that, mother.
I shall be the cloud and you the moon.
I shall cover you with both my hands, and our house-top will be the blue sky.

那些住在波浪中的人民對我喊著——

「我們從早到晚歌唱著；前進，前進，我們旅行著，
不知我們路經什麼地方。」

我問：「不過我怎麼樣來加入你們？」

他們告訴我：「到岸的邊緣來站著，緊閉你的雙眼，
你就會在波浪上被帶去。」

我說：「我母親永遠要我黃昏時在家——我怎能離她
而去呢？」

於是他們笑笑，跳著舞過去了。

但我知道一個比那更好的遊戲。

我將是波浪，你是異鄉的岸。

我要向前滾著，滾著，直到帶著笑聲衝碎在你的膝
上。

世界上沒有人能知道我們兩人在什麼地方。

The folk who live in the waves call out to me—
"We sing from morning till night; on and on we travel
and know not where we pass."
I ask, "But, how am I to join you?"
They tell me, "Come to the edge of the shore and
stand with your eyes tight shut, and you will be carried
out upon the waves."
I say, "My mother always wants me at home in the
evening—how can I leave her and go?"
Then they smile, dance and pass by.
But I know a better game than that.
I will be the waves and you will be a strange shore.
I shall roll on and on and on, and break upon your lap
with laughter.
And no one in the world will know where we both are.

香伯花

假使我變成一朵香伯花，只為好玩，我長在一根樹枝上，高高地在那棵樹上，笑著在風裡搖曳，跳舞在新放芽的葉子上，你會知道我嗎，媽媽？

你要喊：「寶寶，你在那裡？」於是我應該自己竊笑，忍住十分的靜默。

我應該偷偷地開放我的花瓣，看好你在做什麼。

當你沐浴完畢，濡溼的頭髮披在你肩上，你走過香伯樹的影子裡到小庭中去做禱告，你會聞到香伯花的香氣，但不知道是從我發出來的。

當午飯以後你坐在窗前閱讀《羅摩耶那》，樹影子倒在你的頭髮上和膝頭上，我便投我細小的影子在你書頁上，正在你讀著的地方。

但你會猜到這是你孩子的微影嗎？

當黃昏時候，你點著燈在你手裡到牛棚中去，我便驟然再跌落到地上來，仍舊做你的孩子，乞求你講一個故事給我聽。

「你頑皮孩子，你到那裡去了？」

「我不告訴你，媽媽。」這便是你和我要說的。

THE CHAMPA FLOWER

Supposing I became a *champa* flower, just for fun, and grew on a branch high up that tree, and shook in the wind with laughter and danced upon the newly budded leaves, would you know me, mother?

You would call, "Baby, where are you?" and I should laugh to myself and keep quite quiet.

I should slyly open my petals and watch you at your work.

When after your bath, with wet hair spread on your shoulders, you walked through the shadow of the *champa* tree to the little court where you say your prayers, you would notice the scent of the flower, but not know that it came from me.

When after the midday meal you sat at the window reading *Ramayana*, and the tree's shadow fell over your hair and your lap, I should fling my wee little shadow on to the page of your book, just where you were reading.

But would you guess that it was the tiny shadow of your little child?

When in the evening you went to the cowshed with the lighted lamp in your hand, I should suddenly drop on to the earth again and be your own baby once more, and beg you to tell me a story.

"Where have you been, you naughty child?"

"I won't tell you, mother." That's what you and I would say then.

仙　境

假使人們知道了我的國王的宮殿在那裡，宮殿就要消失到空中去。

宮殿的牆壁是白銀做成的，屋頂是發光的金子做成的。

王后住在有七座庭院的王宮裡，她戴一顆寶石，那寶石價值七個國土的財富。

但是讓我來用耳語告訴你，媽媽，我的國王的宮殿在那裡。

它是在我們屋頂花園的角裡一盆吐爾雪植物那兒。

公主睡著在遙遠的七個不能航行的海岸上。

在世界上沒有一個人能找到她，只有我能夠。

她的手上戴著手鐲；她的耳朵上戴著珠子的耳墜。她的頭髮伸展在地上。

她會醒來，當我用我的魔杖觸她。珍珠會從她的嘴唇上滾下來，當她笑的時候。

但是讓我向你耳語，媽媽，她是在那隻角裡，在我們屋頂花園裡的一盆吐爾雪植物那兒。

FAIRYLAND

If people came to know where my king's palace is, it would vanish into the air.

The walls are of white silver and the roof of shining gold.

The queen lives in a palace with seven courtyards, and she wears a jewel that cost all the wealth of seven kingdoms.

But let me tell you, mother, in a whisper, where my king's palace is.

It is at the corner of our terrace where the pot of the *tulsi* plant stands.

———

The princess lies sleeping on the far-away shore of the seven impassable seas.

There is none in the world who can find her but myself.

She has bracelets on her arms and pearl drops in her ears; her hair sweeps down upon the floor.

She will wake when I touch her with my magic wand, and jewels will fall from her lips when she smiles.

But let me whisper in your ear, mother; she is there in the corner of our terrace where the pot of the *tulsi* plant stands.

———

當你要到河裡去洗澡的時候，跨上那屋頂上的花園。

我坐在那角裡，牆頭的影子相連的角裡。

只有貓咪許可和我一起，因為她知道那故事裡的理髮師住在什麼地方。

但是，媽媽，讓我在你耳邊低語，那故事裡的理髮師住在什麼地方。

那是在我們屋頂花園角裡的一盆吐爾雪植物那兒。

When it is time for you to go to the river for your
bath, step up to that terrace on the roof.

I sit in the corner where the shadows of the walls meet
together.

Only puss is allowed to come with me, for she knows
where the barber in the story lives.

But let me whisper, mother, in your ear where the
barber in the story lives.

It is at the corner of the terrace where the pot of the
tulsi plant stands.

放逐之地

媽媽，天空中的光線已經變成灰色；我不知道是什麼時候了。

我的遊戲沒有什麼趣味，所以我到你身邊來。今天星期六，是我們的假日。

放開你的工作，媽媽，坐在這裡靠窗口，告訴我神仙故事中的炭潘泰沙漠在那裡？

━━━◇◇◇◇━━━

雨的陰暗整日覆蓋著。

猛烈的電閃用牠們的爪距搔爬那天空。

當黑雲發出隆隆聲打著雷，我喜歡在我心裡害怕著靠住你。

當密雨整個鐘點的滴瀝在竹葉上，我們的窗子被風狂吹得搖動著發出嘎嘎聲來，我喜歡獨自坐在房中，母親，和你一起，聽你講神仙故事中的炭潘泰沙漠。

━━━◇◇◇◇━━━

THE LAND OF THE EXILE

Mother, the light has grown grey in the sky; I do not know what the time is.

There is no fun in my play, so I have come to you. It is Saturday, our holiday.

Leave off your work, mother; sit here by the window and tell me where the desert of Tepāntar in the fairy tale is?

The shadow of the rains has covered the day from end to end.

The fierce lightning is scratching the sky with its nails.

When the clouds rumble and it thunders, I love to be afraid in my heart and cling to you.

When the heavy rain patters for hours on the bamboo leaves, and our windows shake and rattle at the gusts of wind, I like to sit alone in the room, mother, with you, and hear you talk about the desert of Tepāntar in the fairy tale.

這在那裡，母親，在什麼海的岸上，在什麼山的腳
下，在什麼王的國裡？

那裡沒有籬笆來做田的界線，沒有蹊徑使村人在黃
昏時可以回村，或者在森林裡採薪的婦女可以有路
帶柴薪到市場上去。在沙地裡只有黃草的小叢，只
有一棵樹在炭潘泰沙漠中，有一對聰明的老鳥在那
棵樹上做了窠。

我能夠想像，就在這樣一個暗雲的日子，國王的小
兒子獨自騎上一匹灰馬橫越這沙漠，跋涉那未知的
水去尋覓被禁閉在巨人宮裡的公主。

當雨的陰霾在遠處的天空掛下，電閃爆發像驟然痙
攣的疼痛，他有沒有記起他不幸的母親，被國王所
離棄，掃除著牛棚，揩拭著她的眼睛，當他騎過神
仙故事中的炭潘泰沙漠時？

Where is it, mother, on the shore of what sea, at the foot of what hills, in the kingdom of what king?

There are no hedges there to mark the fields, no footpath across it by which the villagers reach their village in the evening, or the woman who gathers dry sticks in the forest can bring her load to the market. With patches of yellow grass in the sand and only one tree where the pair of wise old birds have their nest, lies the desert of Tepāntar.

I can imagine how, on just such a cloudy day, the young son of the king is riding alone on a grey horse through the desert, in search of the princess who lies imprisoned in the giant's palace across that unknown water.

When the haze of the rain comes down in the distant sky, and lightning starts up like a sudden fit of pain, does he remember his unhappy mother, abandoned by the king, sweeping the cow-stall and wiping her eyes, while he rides through the desert of Tepāntar in the fairy tale?

看，媽媽，在日暮以前天已差不多黑了，已沒有旅
行者在村路上。

牧童早已從牧場回家去，農夫離開他們的農田坐在
他們小屋簷下的蓆上，眼看著頹顏的雲霞。

媽媽，我把我的書本都放在架子上了。——現在不
要催我做功課。

當我長大，長到像父親一樣大，我會把要學的一切
都學會的。

可是就在今天，告訴我，媽媽，神仙故事中的炭潘
泰沙漠在什麼地方？

See, mother, it is almost dark before the day is over, and there are no travellers yonder on the village road.

The shepherd boy has gone home early from the pasture, and men have left their fields to sit on mats under the eaves of their huts, watching the scowling clouds.

Mother, I have left all my books on the shelf—do not ask me to do my lessons now.

When I grow up and am big like my father, I shall learn all that must be learnt.

But just for to-day, tell me, mother, where the desert of Tepāntar in the fairy tale is?

雨　天

陰沉的雲在森林的烏黑邊緣上飛快的聚集。

哦，孩子，不要外出！

那湖邊一排棕櫚樹把他們的頭撞擊那陰鬱的天空；

烏鴉拖曳著翅膀默默地棲在羅望子樹中，而河的東岸被濃重的昏暗所盤據。

我們繫在籬笆上的牛在高聲鳴叫著。

哦，孩子，等在這裡，讓我把牠牽進廄中去。

人們都擠入漲滿水的田地，去捉那些從氾濫的池跳出的魚；雨水似小溪一樣在窄巷中流過，像一個笑著的孩子因要惹惱他的母親而奔跑。

THE RAINY DAY

Sullen clouds are gathering fast over the black fringe of the forest.

O child, do not go out!

The palm trees in a row by the lake are smiting their heads against the dismal sky; the crows with their draggled wings are silent on the tamarind branches, and the eastern bank of the river is haunted by a deepening gloom.

$\infty\!\!\infty\!\!\infty$

Our cow is lowing loud, tied at the fence.

O child, wait here till I bring her into the stall.

Men have crowded into the flooded field to catch the fishes as they escape from the overflowing ponds; the rain water is running in rills through the narrow lanes like a laughing boy who has run away from his mother to tease her.

$\infty\!\!\infty\!\!\infty$

聽啊，有人在渡口呼喊著渡船。

哦，孩子，日光已昏黑，過河的渡船已停息。

天空似乎駕著瘋狂衝襲的雨陣在疾駛，河中的水喧
囂而煩躁，婦人們早已從恆河裡帶著她們盛滿水的
水瓶急忙回家。

黃昏的燈一定要預先做好。

哦，孩子，不要外出！

到市場的路已經無人行走，到河邊去的巷子已經濘
滑不堪。狂風在竹枝間吼叫與掙扎，有如一隻野獸
誘陷在網中。

Listen, someone is shouting for the boatman at the ford.

O child, the daylight is dim, and the crossing at the ferry is closed.

The sky seems to ride fast upon the madly-rushing rain; the water in the river is loud and impatient; women have hastened home early from the Ganges with their filled pitchers.

><><><

The evening lamps must be made ready.

O child, do not go out!

The road to the market is desolate, the lane to the river is slippery. The wind is roaring and struggling among the bamboo branches like a wild beast tangled in a net.

紙　船

一天又一天，我把我的紙船一隻又一隻的漂浮在奔
馳的溪流中。

我用大楷的黑字把我的名字寫在船上，還有我住的
村莊的名字。

我希望在有些陌生地方會有人發見它們，知道我是
誰。

我把我們花園裡的雪麗花載在小船裡，希望這些早
晨的花朵會平安地在晚上帶上岸去。

我把我的紙船放下水，仰望一下天空，看見小雲正
放出他們白色的隆起之帆。

我不知道我的什麼遊伴在天上把他們送下空中來和
我的船競賽！

當夜到來，我埋我的臉在我兩臂間，夢見我的許多
紙船漂浮前進，前進在午夜的星光下。

睡眠的仙人們乘在這些船裡，裝的貨物是他們的籃
子滿載著夢。

PAPER BOATS

Day by day I float my paper boats one by one down the running stream.

In big black letters I write my name on them and the name of the village where I live.

I hope that someone in some strange land will find them and know who I am.

I load my little boats with *shiuli* flowers from our garden, and hope that these blooms of the dawn will be carried safely to land in the night.

I launch my paper boats and look up into the sky and see the little clouds setting their white bulging sails.

I know not what playmate of mine in the sky sends them down the air to race with my boats!

When night comes I bury my face in my arms and dream that my paper boats float on and on under the midnight stars.

The fairies of sleep are sailing in them, and the lading is their baskets full of dreams.

水　手

船夫「馬度」的船碇泊在「刺奇耿奇」碼頭。

這船只無用地裝著些麻，是這樣長久的閒泊在那邊。

只要他願把船借給我，我就供給它一百個划手，升起帆來，五張，六張或七張帆。

我永不駕駛它到愚笨的街市去。

我要航行仙境的七海十三河。

〰〰〰〰〰

不過，媽媽，不要坐在一隻角裡為我而哭泣。

我不是像羅摩旃達羅一樣到森林裡去要等十四年才回來。

我要變成故事裡的王子，把我船裝著喜歡的東西。

我要帶我朋友「阿蘇」同去。我們要歡快地航行仙境的七海十三河。

〰〰〰〰〰

THE SAILOR

The boat of the boatman Madhu is moored at the wharf of Rajgunj.

It is uselessly laden with jute, and has been lying there idle for ever so long.

If he would only lend me his boat, I should man her with a hundred oars, and hoist sails, five or six or seven.

I should never steer her to stupid markets.

I should sail the seven seas and the thirteen rivers of fairyland.

But, mother, you won't weep for me in a corner.

I am not going into the forest like Ramachandra to come back only after fourteen years.

I shall become the prince of the story, and fill my boat with whatever I like.

I shall take my friend Ashu with me. We shall sail merrily across the seven seas and the thirteen rivers of fairyland.

我們要在晨光中起程。

在中午當你在池中沐浴時，我們已到一個陌生國王的領土了。

我們要路經「鐵爾坡尼」津，把炭潘泰沙漠遠離在後面。

我們回來時天要黑了，我就告訴你我所見的一切。

我要橫行仙境的七海十三河。

We shall set sail in the early morning light.

When at noontide you are bathing at the pond, we shall be in the land of a strange king.

We shall pass the ford of Tirpurni, and leave behind us the desert of Tepāntar.

When we come back it will be getting dark, and I shall tell you of all that we have seen.

I shall cross the seven seas and the thirteen rivers of fairyland.

遙遠的彼岸

我渴望到那地方去，到遙遠的彼岸去，

那地方，那些小船繫在竹篙上排成一條線兒；

那地方，在早晨有許多男人跨過他們的小船，肩上
負著犁頭，到他們遠處的田中去；

那地方，牧牛人叫他們鳴噪的牛群游水過河到河邊
的牧場去；

那地方，在傍晚時他們都回家去，剩下那些豺狼的
哀號聲在那荒島的草叢裡。

媽媽，假使你不放在心上，我一定喜歡做那渡頭的
船夫，當我長大以後。

THE FURTHER BANK

I long to go over there to the further bank of the river,
Where those boats are tied to the bamboo poles in a line;
Where men cross over in their boats in the morning with ploughs on their shoulders to till their far-away fields;
Where the cowherds make their lowing cattle swim across to the riverside pasture;
Whence they all come back home in the evening, leaving the jackals to howl in the island overgrown with weeds,
Mother, if you don't mind, I should like to become the boatman of the ferry when I am grown up.

他們說，在那條高高的河岸後面隱蔽著不少奇怪的
水潭，

那地方，成群的野鴨飛來，當雨後的晴天，水潭四
周的邊緣長著深叢的蘆葦，水鳥們就在這裡生蛋；

那地方，群鷸搖擺著牠們的舞尾，印牠們的小足跡
在潔淨的軟泥上；

那地方，在黃昏時候，那些頭戴白花的一片長草邀
請月光漂蕩在他們的波浪上。

媽媽，假使你不放在心上，我一定喜歡做那渡船上
的船夫，當我長大以後。

They say there are strange pools hidden behind that high bank,

Where flocks of wild ducks come when the rains are over, and thick reeds grow round the margins where water-birds lay their eggs;

Where snipes with their dancing tails stamp their tiny footprints upon the clean soft mud;

Where in the evening the tall grasses crested with white flowers invite the moonbeam to float upon their waves.

Mother, if you don't mind, I should like to become the boatman of the ferryboat when I am grown up.

我將搖過去又搖過來，從這邊的河岸到那邊的河岸，那時村上所有的男孩與女孩都要對我驚奇，當他們在河邊沐浴時。

當太陽爬到半空，清晨漸消磨為正午，我將奔跑到你面前來，說：「媽媽，我餓了！」

當白晝完了，影子蜷伏在樹底下，我將在薄暗中回來。

我將永不像父親一樣離開你到城裡去工作。

媽媽，假使你不放在心上，我一定喜歡做那渡船上的船夫，當我長大以後。

I shall cross and cross back from bank to bank, and all the boys and girls of the village will wonder at me while they are bathing.

When the sun climbs the mid sky and morning wears on to noon, I shall come running to you, saying, "Mother, I am hungry!"

When the day is done and the shadows cower under the trees, I shall come back in the dusk.

I shall never go away from you into the town to work like father.

Mother, if you don't mind, I should like to become the boatman of the ferryboat when I am grown up.

花 校

當烏雲在天空發出隆隆聲，六月的陣雨就開始了，
潮溼的東風行經荒原，在竹林中來吹他的風笛。
那時群花就突然從無人知道的地方出來，狂歡地在
草地上舞蹈。

母親，我真正相信花兒是到地下上學去的。
他們把門關著讀書，若是他們要未到時間就出來玩
耍，他們的教師就要叫他們立壁角的。

THE FLOWER-SCHOOL

When storm clouds rumble in the sky and June showers come down,
The moist east wind comes marching over the heath to blow its bagpipes among the bamboos.
Then crowds of flowers come out of a sudden, from nobody knows where, and dance upon the grass in wild glee.

Mother, I really think the flowers go to school underground.
They do their lessons with doors shut, and if they want to come out to play before it is time, their master makes them stand in a corner.

當雨季到來，他們就放假了。

森林的枝條相擊，在野風中葉子發沙沙聲，雷雲們
拍著他們巨大的手，花朵孩童們就衝出來了，穿著
粉紅、鵝黃與雪白服裝。

———〰〰〰———

你知道嗎，母親，他們的家在天上，就是有星星的
地方。

你有沒有看見他們是怎樣急切的要到那裡去？你是
不是知道他們為什麼這樣的匆急？

當然，我能猜得出他們對誰高舉著他們的兩臂：他
們有他們的母親，像我有我的一樣。

When the rains come they have their holidays.

Branches clash together in the forest, and the leaves rustle in the wild wind, the thunder-clouds clap their giant hands and the flower children rush out in dresses of pink and yellow and white.

∽∽∽∽∽

Do you know, mother, their home is in the sky, where the stars are.

Haven't you seen how eager they are to get there? Don't you know why they are in such a hurry?

Of course, I can guess to whom they raise their arms: they have their mother as I have my own.

商　人

媽媽，設想你住在家裡，我旅行遠赴異鄉。

設想我的小船已經停在碼頭滿裝著貨物。

現在，好好兒想，媽媽，你說什麼我便帶給你，當
我回來的時候。

※

媽媽，你要不要一堆一堆的黃金？

那裡，在金河的岸邊，田地中滿是黃金的收穫。

還有森林蔭翳的路上金黃的香伯花落到地上來。

我將把它們聚集起來一起給你，裝滿千百隻的筐子。

※

THE MERCHANT

Imagine, mother, that you are to stay at home and I am to travel into strange lands.

Imagine that my boat is ready at the landing fully laden.

Now think well, mother, before you say what I shall bring for you when I come back.

〜〜〜

Mother, do you want heaps and heaps of gold?

There, by the banks of golden streams, fields are full of golden harvest.

And in the shade of the forest path the golden *champa* flowers drop on the ground.

I will gather them all for you in many hundred baskets.

〜〜〜

媽媽，你要不要像秋天雨點一樣大的珍珠？

我將經過珍珠島的海岸。

那裡在日出的晨光中珍珠在草地的花卉上顫動，珍珠落在草上，珍珠給撒野的海浪噴散在沙上。

我的哥哥會有一對生翼的馬兒可以飛在雲端裡。

給父親呢，我會帶來一枝魔筆，用不到他的知曉，筆自己會寫字。

給你呢，媽媽，我一定有小箱子與那珠寶，價值七個國王他們的國土。

Mother, do you want pearls big as the raindrops of autumn?

I shall cross to the pearl island shore.

There in the early morning light pearls tremble on the meadow flowers, pearls drop on the grass, and pearls are scattered on the sand in spray by the wild sea-waves.

My brother shall have a pair of horses with wings to fly among the clouds.

For father I shall bring a magic pen that, without his knowing, will write of itself.

For you, mother, I must have the casket and jewel that cost seven kings their kingdoms.

同　情

假使我只是一隻小狗，不是你的孩兒，親愛的媽，
你要不要對我說「不」，當我要從你的碟中來吃東
西？
你是不是要把我趕走，對我說著，「滾開，你頑皮的
小狗」？
那麼，去吧，媽，去吧！我將永不理睬你，不管你
怎麼樣叫我，而且我將永不讓你來餵我一些。

〰〰〰〰〰

假使我只是一隻小小的綠色鸚鵡，不是你的孩兒，
親愛的媽，你要不要怕我飛去而把我用鏈鎖牢？
你是不是要對我擺著手指說：「一隻多麼可鄙的忘恩
鳥！牠日夜在咬牠的鎖鏈？」
那麼，去吧，媽，去吧！我要逃到森林中去了；我
將永不再讓你抱我在懷中。

SYMPATHY

If I were only a little puppy, not your baby, mother dear, would you say "No" to me if I tried to eat from your dish?

Would you drive me off, saying to me, "Get away, you naughty little puppy"?

Then go, mother, go! I will never come to you when you call me, and never let you feed me any more.

If I were only a little green parrot, and not your baby, mother dear, would you keep me chained lest I should fly away?

Would you shake your finger at me and say, "What an ungrateful wretch of a bird! It is gnawing at its chain day and night?"

Then, go, mother, go! I will run away into the woods; I will never let you take me in your arms again.

職　業

早晨鐘響十下時，我沿著我們那條巷走向學校，

每天我逢到那小販喊著：「手鐲，水晶手鐲！」

沒有什麼使他匆促，沒有他一定要走的路，沒有地方他必須要去，沒有他必須回家的時間。

我願我是一個小販，整天消磨在路上，喊著：「手鐲，水晶手鐲！」

下午四時我從學校回家，

我能從那間屋子的大門看見花匠在掘地。

他用他的鑱做他喜歡的工作，他把自己的衣服塗滿了塵埃，沒有人來責備他，如果他在太陽裡燻曬或被雨水打溼。

我願我是一個花匠，在園中掘土，沒有人來阻止我。

VOCATION

When the gong sounds ten in the morning and I walk
to school by our lane,
Every day I meet the hawker crying, "Bangles, crystal
bangles!"
There is nothing to hurry him on, there is no road he
must take, no place he must go to, no time when he
must come home.
I wish I were a hawker, spending my day in the road,
crying, "Bangles, crystal bangles!"

When at four in the afternoon I come back from the
school,
I can see through the gate of that house the gardener
digging the ground.
He does what he likes with his spade, he soils his
clothes with dust, nobody takes him to task if he gets
baked in the sun or gets wet.
I wish I were a gardener digging away at the garden
with nobody to stop me from digging.

就在傍晚天黑，母親叫我去睡覺時，

我可以從開著的窗中看見那更夫來去地踱著。

巷裡黑暗而寂寞，街燈站在那裡像一個巨人，他的頭上有一隻紅眼睛。

更夫晃著他的燈籠，他的影子跟在他旁邊一起走著，他生平從沒有一次到床上去過。

我願我是一個更夫，整夜在街上踱著，帶著我的燈籠追趕那影子。

Just as it gets dark in the evening and my mother
sends me to bed,

I can see through my open window the watchman
walking up and down.

The lane is dark and lonely, and the street-lamp
stands like a giant with one red eye in its head.

The watchman swings his lantern and walks with his
shadow at his side, and never once goes to bed in his
life.

I wish I were a watchman walking the streets all night,
chasing the shadows with my lantern.

年長者

媽媽，你的孩兒是這樣的笨！她是怎樣可笑的孩子氣啊！

她不知道路上的燈光與星的光有什麼不同。

當我們玩耍吃卵石，她想它們是真的食物要想把它們放在她的嘴裡。

當我揭開一本書在她面前叫她學她的 a、b、c，她用她的手將書頁撕碎，發出快樂的聲音，不當什麼一回事。這是你的孩兒做她的功課的方法。

當我發怒對她搖搖頭，罵她頑皮，她就大笑，以為很有趣。

大家知道父親出去了，但是如果在玩耍時我喊著「爸爸」，她就看來看去很興奮，以為父親就在附近。

當我在那洗衣服人帶來的驢子班上上課，我警告她，我是校長。她無緣無故地尖聲怪叫，還是叫我哥哥。

你的孩兒要想捉住月兒，她是多麼滑稽，她把象頭神叫做強頭神。

媽媽，你的孩子是這樣的笨，她是怎麼樣可笑的孩子氣啊！

SUPERIOR

Mother, your baby is silly! She is so absurdly childish!
She does not know the difference between the lights
in the streets and the stars.

When we play at eating with pebbles, she thinks they
are real food, and tries to put them into her mouth.

When I open a book before her and ask her to learn
her a, b, c, she tears the leaves with her hands and
roars for joy at nothing; this is your baby's way of
doing her lesson.

When I shake my head at her in anger and scold her
and call her naughty, she laughs and thinks it great
fun.

Everybody knows that father is away, but if in play I
call aloud "Father," she looks about her in excitement
and thinks that father is near.

When I hold my class with the donkeys that our
washerman brings to carry away the clothes and I warn
her that I am the schoolmaster, she will scream for no
reason and call me dādā.

Your baby wants to catch the moon. She is so funny;
she calls Ganesh Gānush.

Mother, your baby is silly, she is so absurdly childish!

小大人

我是小的，因為我是一個小孩子，我會變成高大，當我像父親一樣年紀。

我的先生走來對我說：「現在不早了，拿你的石板和書來。」

我就要告訴他：「你不知道我已經和父親一樣大了嗎？我一定不必再讀什麼書了。」

我的先生就要驚奇地說：「他可以不讀書，如果他歡喜，因為他已經長大了。」

<hr>

我要盛裝了我自己到市場去，那裡的人群密集著。

我的伯父就要衝上來說：「你要迷失的，我的孩子；讓我來抱你。」

我就要回答：「你有沒有看見，伯父，我已經和父親一樣大了。我一定要獨自到市場去。」

伯父就要說：「是的，他喜歡到那裡去，他就可以到那裡去，因為他已經長大了。」

<hr>

THE LITTLE BIG MAN

I am small because I am a little child. I shall be big when I am as old as my father is.

My teacher will come and say, "It is late, bring your slate and your books."

I shall tell him, "Do you not know I am as big as father? And I must not have lessons any more."

My master will wonder and say, "He can leave his books if he likes, for he is grown up."

I shall dress myself and walk to the fair where the crowd is thick.

My uncle will come rushing up to me and say, "You will get lost, my boy; let me carry you."

I shall answer, "Can't you see, uncle, I am as big as father. I must go to the fair alone."

Uncle will say, "Yes, he can go wherever he likes, for he is grown up."

母親將從她的沐場回來,知道我要把錢給我的保姆,
因為我問著怎樣把我的鑰匙開箱子。

母親就要說:「你在做什麼事,頑皮孩子?」

我就要告訴她:「媽媽,你不知道我已經和父親一樣
大了嗎。我一定要拿銀子給我的保姆。」

母親就要對自己說:「他可以喜歡把錢給誰便給誰,
因為他已經長大了。」

在十月的假期裡,父親要回家來,他想我仍舊是個
嬰孩,就要從城裡帶給我小鞋子和小絲衣。

我就要說:「爸爸,把這些給我的哥哥,因為我已經
和你一樣大了。」

父親就要想著說:「他可以買自己的衣服,如果他歡
喜,因為他是長大了。」

Mother will come from her bath when I am giving money to my nurse, for I shall know how to open the box with my key.

Mother will say, "What are you about, naughty child?"

I shall tell her, "Mother, don't you know, I am as big as father, and I must give silver to my nurse."

Mother will say to herself, "He can give money to whom he likes, for he is grown up."

━━◇◇◇◇◇━━

In the holiday time in October father will come home and, thinking that I am still a baby, will bring for me from the town little shoes and small silken frocks.

I shall say, "Father, give them to my dādā, for I am as big as you are."

Father will think and say, "He can buy his own clothes if he likes, for he is grown up."

十二點鐘

媽媽，我現在不要再做功課了，我已經讀了一早晨的書了。

你說現在還不過只十二點鐘。假使這鐘沒有一點兒慢，那麼，實在只是十二點鐘，但你為什麼不能當做是午後呢？

我能很容易地想像，現在那太陽已經落在那稻田的邊緣了，還有那個賣魚的老婦人在池塘邊採集草頭做晚飯。

我能閉上我的眼睛就想起那黑影在「瑪大」樹下慢慢地濃起來，還有那池塘裡的水看起來有著黑色的光澤。

如果十二點鐘能在晚上來，為什麼晚上不能在十二點鐘來呢？

TWELVE O'CLOCK

Mother, I do want to leave off my lessons now. I have been at my book all the morning.

You say it is only twelve o'clock. Suppose it isn't any later; can't you ever think it is afternoon when it is only twelve o'clock?

I can easily imagine now that the sun has reached the edge of that rice-field, and the old fisher-woman is gathering herbs for her supper by the side of the pond.

I can just shut my eyes and think that the shadows are growing darker under the *madar* tree, and the water in the pond looks shiny black.

If twelve o'clock can come in the night, why can't the night come when it is twelve o'clock?

寫 作

你說父親寫許多書，但是他寫的什麼我都不懂。

他一黃昏都在讀給你聽，但是你真的能辨出他說的是什麼意思嗎？

媽媽，你能告訴我們，多麼有趣的故事！我奇怪為什麼父親不能那樣寫？

是不是他從來沒有在自己的母親那裡聽到巨人、仙人和公主的故事？

是不是他都忘記了？

〜〜〜〜〜

常常當他遲來洗澡時，你就要去叫他一百遍。

你等他，把他吃的東西弄熱，但是他只管寫下去，忘記了。

父親一向在玩著著書。

無論何時我到父親的房間裡去玩，你就要來對我說：「多麼頑皮的孩子！」

如果我發出小小的聲音，你就說：「你沒有看見父親在做事嗎？」

常常寫字有什麼趣味？

〜〜〜〜〜

AUTHORSHIP

You say that father writes a lot of books, but what he writes I don't understand.

He was reading to you all the evening, but could you really make out what he meant?

What nice stories, mother, you can tell us! Why can't father write like that, I wonder?

Did he never hear from his own mother stories of giants and fairies and princesses?

Has he forgotten them all?

Often when he gets late for his bath you have to go and call him an hundred times.

You wait and keep his dishes warm for him, but he goes on writing and forgets.

Father always plays at making books.

If ever I go to play in father's room, you come and call me, "What a naughty child!"

If I make the slightest noise, you say, "Don't you see that father's at his work?"

What's the fun of always writing and writing?

當我拿起父親的鋼筆或鉛筆來，就像他一樣的在他
的書上寫 a、b、c、d、e、f、g、h、i，為什麼你就
要對我光火，媽媽？

你一句話都不說，當父親在寫稿子。

當父親浪費這樣一大堆紙，媽媽，你似乎一點都不
在乎。

可是，我不過拿一張紙做隻船，你就說：「孩子，你
多麼討厭啊！」

不知你怎樣想法，對於父親的損壞一張又一張的紙，
把兩面都寫著黑色的記號？

When I take up father's pen or pencil and write upon his book just as he does,—a, b, c, d, e, f, g, h, i,—why do you get cross with me, then, mother?

You never say a word when father writes.

When my father wastes such heaps of paper, mother, you don't seem to mind at all.

But if I take only one sheet to make a boat with, you say, "Child, how troublesome you are!"

What do you think of father's spoiling sheets and sheets of paper with black marks all over on both sides?

可惡的郵差

為什麼你很靜寂，很沉默地坐在那裡地板上？告訴我，親愛的媽媽。

雨從開著的窗子外面進來，把你滿身落溼了，但是你不放在心上。

你沒有聽到那時鐘敲四點嗎？這是我哥哥要從學校回來的時候了。

你遇到什麼事了？為什麼你看起來很冷淡？

今天你收到一封父親寄來的信嗎？

我看見那郵差在鎮上送他郵袋裡的信，幾幾乎每一個人家都有了。

只有父親的信他放起來自己讀，我斷定那郵差是個壞人。

但是不要因為這事便不快樂，親愛的媽媽。

明天鄰村是趕集的日子，你叫你的女僕去買點紙筆來。

我自己來寫許多父親的信；你會找不出一點兒錯處。

我要從 A 一直寫到 K。

但是媽媽，你為什麼要笑？

THE WICKED POSTMAN

Why do you sit there on the floor so quiet and silent, tell me, mother dear?

The rain is coming in through the open window, making you all wet, and you don't mind it.

Do you hear the gong striking four? It is time for my brother to come home from school.

What has happened to you that you look so strange?

Haven't you got a letter from father to-day?

I saw the postman bringing letters in his bag for almost everybody in the town.

Only, father's letters he keeps to read himself. I am sure the postman is a wicked man.

But don't be unhappy about that, mother dear.

To-morrow is market day in the next village. You ask your maid to buy some pens and papers.

I myself will write all father's letters; you will not find a single mistake.

I shall write from A right up to K.

But, mother, why do you smile?

難道你不相信我能寫得像父親一樣好嗎！

但是我要小小心心地把我的紙劃線，就把許多字母都寫得美麗地巨大。

當我寫完了，你是不是以為我要像父親那樣笨得把牠們放在那個可惡郵差的郵袋裡去呢？

我要自己把信送給你，不必等待，我就一字字的幫你讀我的信。

我知道那個郵差不願意送給你真正的好信。

You don't believe that I can write as nicely as father does!

But I shall rule my paper carefully, and write all the letters beautifully big.

When I finish my writing, do you think I shall be so foolish as father and drop it into the horrid postman's bag?

I shall bring it to you myself without waiting, and letter by letter help you to read my writing.

I know the postman does not like to give you the really nice letters.

英　雄

媽媽，讓我們想像我們在旅行中，途經一個奇異而
危險的國家。

你坐在一頂轎子裡，我騎著一匹紅馬跟著你。

傍晚的時候，太陽正西沉，「喬拉提奇」荒地的一片
灰白色展開在我們前面。那地區荒瘠而無人煙。

你驚怖地想著——「我不知道我們到了什麼地方
了。」

我對你說：「媽媽，不要害怕。」

那草原都是針刺的鐵釘草，通過這裡只有一條湮沒
了的狹徑。

那地方，田野間不見牲口；那牛群已到村上的牛棚
裡去了。

天暗下來了，地上也墨黑，我們不能說出我們在向
那裡走。

你忽然喊我，低低地問我：「這是什麼光，在靠近那
岸邊？」

THE HERO

Mother, let us imagine we are travelling, and passing through a strange and dangerous country.

You are riding in a palanquin and I am trotting by you on a red horse.

It is evening and the sun goes down. The waste of Joradighi lies wan and grey before us. The land is desolate and barren.

You are frightened and thinking—"I know not where we have come to."

I say to you, "Mother, do not be afraid."

<hr/>

The meadow is prickly with spiky grass, and through it runs a narrow broken path.

There are no cattle to be seen in the wide field; they have gone to their village stalls.

It grows dark and dim on the land and sky, and we cannot tell where we are going.

Suddenly you call me and ask me in a whisper, "What light is that near the bank?"

<hr/>

就在這當兒，一個可怖的喊聲迸發出來，一群人馬奔跑著向我們衝來。

你蹲伏在轎子裡，口中喃喃地禱告，背誦諸神的名字。

轎夫們驚駭到顫慄著，都躲到荊棘中藏匿起來。

我對你喊道：「不要怕，媽媽，有我在這裡。」

他們手裡都拿著長棒，頭上的頭髮是散亂的。他們近來了，近來了。

我高喊：「當心，你們惡棍！再走上一步，要你們的命。」

他們又一陣可怕的吶喊，便向前衝鋒。

你緊握著我的手說：「親愛的孩子，千萬不要冒失，你避開他們。」

我說：「媽媽，你看我就得了。」

Just then there bursts out a fearful yell, and figures come running towards us.

You sit crouched in your palanquin and repeat the names of the gods in prayer.

The bearers, shaking in terror, hide themselves in the thorny bush.

I shout to you, "Don't be afraid, mother. I am here."

⋙⋘

With long sticks in their hands and hair all wild about their heads, they come nearer and nearer.

I shout, "Have a care, you villains! One step more and you are dead men."

They give another terrible yell and rush forward.

You clutch my hand and say, "Dear boy, for heaven's sake, keep away from them."

I say, "Mother, just you watch me."

⋙⋘

於是，我策動我的馬疾馳，我的劍與盾鏗鏗作聲，
和他們互擊。

戰鬥進行得十分可怖，媽媽，你在轎子裡看見了，
會使你一陣寒顫。

許多人逃竄了，一大批人斬成一塊塊的。

我知道你呆坐在那裡，你在想，你的孩子這時一定
被殺了。

可是我卻到你身邊來了，滿身染著鮮血，我說：「媽
媽，現在打完了。」

你走出轎子來吻我，把我緊抱在心口，你自言自語
的說：

「我不知道我該怎麼辦？如果沒有我的孩子護送
我。」

千千萬萬無謂的事情一天天發生著，為什麼不能有
機會真的來一椿這樣的事情呢？

這會好像書裡的一個故事的。

我的哥哥會說：「這是可能的嗎？我一向想他是這樣
的柔弱！」

我們莊上的人就都要驚愕地說：「這不是很幸運的
嗎，有這男孩伴著他的母親？」

Then I spur my horse for a wild gallop, and my sword and buckler clash against each other.

The fight becomes so fearful, mother, that it would give you a cold shudder could you see it from your palanquin.

Many of them fly, and a great number are cut to pieces.

I know you are thinking, sitting all by yourself, that your boy must be dead by this time.

But I come to you all stained with blood, and say, "Mother, the fight is over now."

You come out and kiss me, pressing me to your heart, and you say to yourself,

"I don't know what I should do if I hadn't my boy to escort me."

A thousand useless things happen day after day, and why couldn't such a thing come true by chance?

It would be like a story in a book.

My brother would say, "Is it possible? I always thought he was so delicate!"

Our village people would all say in amazement, "Was it not lucky that the boy was with his mother?"

終　結

現在是我去的時候了，媽媽，我去了。

在寂寞的黎明之魚肚白的黑暗中當你在床上伸出你的兩臂來抱你的孩兒，我將說：「孩兒不在那裡！」——媽媽，我去了。

我將變成清風來撫愛你；當你沐浴時我將成水中的微波，吻著你，又吻著你。

在狂風的夜裡，當雨點落在葉上起聲時，你在你床上將聽到我的低語，而我的笑聲將跟著閃電在開著的窗中同進你房中。

如果你想念你的孩兒而且到夜深不寐，我將從星斗中對你唱：「睡吧，媽媽，睡吧。」

你睡著時，我將在流蕩的月光中偷偷地來到你的床上，躺在你懷抱裡。

我將變成一個夢，溜進你眼瞼微合的隙縫中，深入你睡眠之境；當你醒來驚恐地探視你周圍，我就飛出來像閃光的螢火掠入黑暗中。

當那盛大的「普佳」節到來，鄰人的孩子們都來屋子四周玩耍，我要溶化在笛的樂聲中，整天在你心中震盪著。

親愛的姨母將帶著「普佳」的禮物來問：「姐姐，我們的孩兒呢？」媽媽，那麼你輕輕地對她說：「他在我的瞳人中，他在我的身體中，我的靈魂中。」

THE END

It is time for me to go, mother; I am going.

When in the paling darkness of the lonely dawn you stretch out your arms for your baby in the bed, I shall say, "Baby is not there!"—mother, I am going.

I shall become a delicate draught of air and caress you; and I shall be ripples in the water when you bathe, and kiss you and kiss you again.

In the gusty night when the rain patters on the leaves you will hear my whisper in your bed, and my laughter will flash with the lightning through the open window into your room.

If you lie awake, thinking of your baby till late into the night, I shall sing to you from the stars, "Sleep, mother, sleep."

On the straying moonbeams I shall steal over your bed, and lie upon your bosom while you sleep.

I shall become a dream, and through the little opening of your eyelids I shall slip into the depths of your sleep; and when you wake up and look round startled, like a twinkling firefly I shall flit out into the darkness.

When, on the great festival of *puja*, the neighbours' children come and play about the house, I shall melt into the music of the flute and throb in your heart all day.

Dear auntie will come with *puja*-presents and will ask, "Where is our baby, sister?" Mother, you will tell her softly, "He is in the pupils of my eyes, he is in my body and in my soul."

招　魂

她離開的時候，夜是黑漆漆的，他們都睡熟了。
現在夜是黑的，我叫喚著她：「歸來啊，我的寶貝；
世界睡著了，星星默默地望著星星，如果你回來一
刻，沒有人會知道的。」

～～～～

她離開的時候，樹林剛放芽，春天還年輕。
現在花朵已盛放，我呼喚著：「歸來啊，我的寶貝。
孩子們隨意玩耍，把花朵採集了又灑開。如果你來
拿一朵小花，沒有人會覺察的。」

～～～～

那些玩耍的人，仍在玩耍，生命是這樣的被浪費。
我聽著他們的喋喋談話聲而叫喚：「歸來啊，我的寶
貝，母親的心充滿著愛，如果你來向她偷一個小小
的吻沒有人會妒忌的。」

THE RECALL

The night was dark when she went away, and they slept.

The night is dark now, and I call for her, "Come back, my darling; the world is asleep; and no one would know, if you came for a moment while stars are gazing at stars."

∽∽∽

She went away when the trees were in bud and the spring was young.

Now the flowers are in high bloom and I call, "Come back, my darling. The children gather and scatter flowers in reckless sport. And if you come and take one little blossom no one will miss it."

∽∽∽

Those that used to play are playing still, so spendthrift is life.

I listen to their chatter and call, "Come back, my darling, for mother's heart is full to the brim with love, and if you come to snatch only one little kiss from her no one will grudge it."

第一次的茉莉花

啊，這些茉莉花，這些白色的茉莉花！

我似乎還記得當我把我兩手捧著這些茉莉花的第一
天，這些白色的茉莉花。

我愛過那陽光，那蒼天和綠色的大地；

我聽見過在子夜的黑暗中飄著的河水之流瀉的淙
淙；

秋天的落日，在寂寞的荒野的路彎向我迎來，像一
個新娘舉起她的面幕來接受她的愛人。

但是我的記憶仍為我兒時第一次手執的幾朵白茉莉
花而芬芳。

在我的生命中帶來了好多歡快的日子，在節日的夜
裡，我曾同尋樂的人們笑語。

在雨的灰色之晨，我低唱過好多一隻一隻的閒歌。

我在我頸上戴了愛之手所織的鈠古拉的黃昏花環。

但是我的心是甜蜜的，當我記憶起那些在我兒時，
第一次捧在我手裡的幾朵新鮮的茉莉花。

THE FIRST JASMINES

Ah, these jasmines, these white jasmines!

I seem to remember the first day when I filled my hands with these jasmines, these white jasmines.

I have loved the sunlight, the sky and the green earth;

I have heard the liquid murmur of the river through the darkness of midnight;

Autumn sunsets have come to me at the bend of a road in the lonely waste, like a bride raising her veil to accept her lover.

Yet my memory is still sweet with the first white jasmines that I held in my hand when I was a child.

∞

Many a glad day has come in my life, and I have laughed with merrymakers on festival nights.

On grey mornings of rain I have crooned many an idle song.

I have worn round my neck the evening wreath of *bakulas* woven by the hand of love.

Yet my heart is sweet with the memory of the first fresh jasmines that filled my hands when I was a child.

榕　樹

啊，枝枒參差的榕樹，站在池塘岸上，你有沒有忘記那小孩子，像那些鳥兒一樣在你枝葉間巢居而又飛去了的小孩？

你記得嗎？他坐在窗口，驚奇地望著你那些向地下投陷的根之糾纏。

女人們帶著水瓶到池裡來汲水，而你巨大的黑陰就開始在水面蠕動，像睡眠掙扎著要醒來。

日光在水波上舞蹈，像不息地梭織著金色的繡帷。

兩隻鴨子游過垂影下來的草叢的邊緣，那孩子就靜坐著沉思。

他渴想著要變成風來吹過你的沙沙發聲的枝枒，變成你的陰影，跟著日光在水上伸延，變成一隻鳥棲息在你最高的枝上，或像那些鴨子在雜草與陰影中漂浮。

THE BANYAN TREE

O you shaggy-headed banyan tree standing on the bank of the pond, have you forgotten the little child, like the birds that have nested in your branches and left you?

Do you not remember how he sat at the window and wondered at the tangle of your roots that plunged underground?

The women would come to fill their jars in the pond, and your huge black shadow would wriggle on the water like sleep struggling to wake up.

Sunlight danced on the ripples like restless tiny shuttles weaving golden tapestry.

Two ducks swam by the weedy margin above their shadows, and the child would sit still and think.

He longed to be the wind and blow through your rustling branches, to be your shadow and lengthen with the day on the water, to be a bird and perch on your topmost twig, and to float like those ducks among the weeds and shadows.

祝　福

祝福於這顆小心，這潔白的靈魂，他給我們的大地
贏得了天空的吻。

他愛太陽的光明，他愛看母親的臉。

他沒有學得去輕蔑塵埃，去渴望黃金。

緊抱他在你心裡，祝福他。

他來到這有成百十字路的地方。

我不知道他為什麼從群眾中挑選你，到你門前來，
緊握住你的手問他的路。

他會跟隨著你，有說有笑，心中不存絲毫懷疑。

保守他的信心，領他走正路，並祝福他。

把你的手放在他頭頂，祈禱：雖然底下的浪濤在增
加狂暴，但上面的風也會來把他的帆張滿，吹他到
平安之港。

別在你匆忙中忘卻他，讓他到你心裡來，祝福他吧。

BENEDICTION

Bless this little heart, this white soul that has won the kiss of heaven for our earth.

He loves the light of the sun, he loves the sight of his mother's face.

He has not learned to despise the dust, and to hanker after gold.

Clasp him to your heart and bless him.

He has come into this land of an hundred cross-roads.

I know not how he chose you from the crowd, came to your door, and grasped your hand to ask his way.

He will follow you, laughing and talking, and not a doubt in his heart.

Keep his trust, lead him straight and bless him.

Lay your hand on his head, and pray that though the waves underneath grow threatening, yet the breath from above may come and fill his sails and waft him to the haven of peace.

Forget him not in your hurry, let him come to your heart and bless him.

禮　物

我的孩子，我要給你樣東西，因為我們在世界的河流上漂泊。

我們的生命能被分散，而我們的愛被忘卻。

但我並不笨拙到希望能用禮物來買你的心。

你還年幼，你的路是長的，你一口喝乾了我們給你的愛，轉身跑開了。

你有你的玩耍，你有你的遊伴，如果你沒有時間或心思來伴我們，那對我們有什麼傷害。

是的，我們年老了，有空閒來數過去的光陰，在我們的心裡撫愛那我們的手已經永遠失去的東西。

河流歌唱著向前疾進，衝破一切的障礙。但那山岳卻留在那裡，憶念著她，用他的愛跟隨她的前程。

THE GIFT

I want to give you something, my child, for we are drifting in the stream of the world.

Our lives will be carried apart, and our love forgotten.

But I am not so foolish as to hope that I could buy your heart with my gifts.

Young is your life, your path long, and you drink the love we bring you at one draught and turn and run away from us.

You have your play and your playmates. What harm is there if you have no time or thought for us.

We, indeed, have leisure enough in old age to count the days that are past, to cherish in our hearts what our hands have lost for ever.

The river runs swift with a song, breaking through all barriers. But the mountain stays and remembers, and follows her with his love.

我的歌

我的孩子，這首我的歌將揚起樂聲像愛之歡欣的手臂來盤繞你。

這首我的歌將如一個祝福的吻撫觸你的額頭。

當你獨自時我的歌會坐在你旁邊在你耳中低語。當你在眾人之間，我的歌會用超然來守衛你。

我的歌將如你夢的雙翼，運送你的心到未知的邊緣去。

我的歌將如忠心的星照在你頭上，當黑夜隱沒了你的道路。

我的歌將坐在你眼睛的瞳人裡帶你的視線看進東西的心裡去。

還有，當我的聲音在死亡中靜止，我的歌會在你活著的心中言語。

MY SONG

This song of mine will wind its music around you, my child, like the fond arms of love.

This song of mine will touch your forehead like a kiss of blessing.

When you are alone it will sit by your side and whisper in your ear, when you are in the crowd it will fence you about with aloofness.

My song will be like a pair of wings to your dreams, it will transport your heart to the verge of the unknown.

It will be like the faithful star overhead when dark night is over your road.

My song will sit in the pupils of your eyes, and will carry your sight into the heart of things.

And when my voice is silent in death, my song will speak in your living heart.

小天使

他們喧鬧，他們格鬥，他們猜疑與失望，他們爭吵著不知終結。

我的孩子，讓你的生命到他們當中去，像光明的火焰，安定而純潔，你使他們快樂得靜默下來。

他們殘暴地貪婪著，嫉妒著，他們的言辭有如隱藏的刀，正渴於飲血。

去，我的孩子，去站在他們不歡之心的中間，讓你溫和的眼睛落在他們身上，有如黃昏的慈愛之和平蓋沒那日間的爭擾。

讓他們看你的臉，我的孩子，因而知道一切事物的意義；讓他們愛你，因而彼此相愛。

來，我的孩子，坐在無限的懷抱裡，在日出時開啟而振作你的心，有如一朵開放的花，在日落時，垂下你的頭，在靜默中完成這一天的禮拜。

THE CHILD-ANGEL

They clamour and fight, they doubt and despair, they know no end to their wranglings.

Let your life come amongst them like a flame of light, my child, unflickering and pure, and delight them into silence.

They are cruel in their greed and their envy, their words are like hidden knives thirsting for blood.

Go and stand amidst their scowling hearts, my child, and let your gentle eyes fall upon them like the forgiving peace of the evening over the strife of the day.

Let them see your face, my child, and thus know the meaning of all things; let them love you and thus love each other.

Come and take your seat in the bosom of the limitless, my child. At sunrise open and raise your heart like a blossoming flower, and at sunset bend your head and in silence complete the worship of the day.

最後的交易

「來啊，來僱用我。」我叫喊著，早晨我在石子鋪的路上行走。

劍在手，國王在他的戰車中到來。

他拉著我的手說：「我用我的權力來僱用你。」

但是他的權力全無價值，他乘著他的戰車走了。

日中的暑熱裡，那些屋子都關著門。

我在一條曲巷裡漫行。

一個老者提著一袋黃金出來。

他考慮了一下說：「我用金錢來僱用你。」

他一個一個地計算他的錢幣，我回轉身來走了。

日中的暑熱裡，那些屋子都關著門。

那是黃昏，花園的籬笆盛開著花。

一個美女出來說：「我用笑來僱用你。」

她的笑容淡下來融成眼淚，她獨自回到黑暗中去了。

THE LAST BARGAIN

"Come and hire me," I cried, while in the morning I was walking on the stone-paved road.

Sword in hand, the King came in his chariot.

He held my hand and said, "I will hire you with my power."

But his power counted for nought, and he went away in his chariot.

In the heat of the midday the houses stood with shut doors.

I wandered along the crooked lane.

An old man came out with his bag of gold.

He pondered and said, "I will hire you with my money."

He weighed his coins one by one, but I turned away.

It was evening. The garden hedge was all aflower.

The fair maid came out and said, "I will hire you with a smile."

Her smile paled and melted into tears, and she went back alone into the dark.

太陽在沙灘上閃光，海波任性地破碎成浪花。

一個孩子坐著玩弄貝殼。

他仰起頭來，似乎認得我地說：「我用無物僱用你。」

從那時起，那交易就在孩子的遊戲中成功，使我成為自由人。

The sun glistened on the sand, and the sea waves broke waywardly.

A child sat playing with shells.

He raised his head and seemed to know me, and said, "I hire you with nothing."

From thenceforward that bargain struck in child's play made me a free man.

譯者附註

本書內〈仙境〉、〈年長者〉、〈小大人〉、〈十二點鐘〉、〈寫作〉、〈可惡的郵差〉等六篇為麋鳳麗女士所譯。

泰戈爾小說戲劇集
糜文開　裴普賢　譯

階級、宗教與國家，誰能帶來終極正義？
這把「戀之火」若燒得過國族與宗教的藩籬，能否看到
「奚德蘿」的永恆真我？還是剩下「骷髏」般的寡婦軀
體，為受莫名的歧視，而暗自泣血？
在道德與自我之間，誰來成全我們的愛情？
心愛的人就在眼前，是什麼阻止我伸手擁抱？就讓時間
駐留在這「無上的一夜」吧！

印度文學欣賞（二版）
糜文開　著

印度文化以宗教為核心，印度歷史就等於一部宗教的演
變史，而印度文學史也就可依宗教的演變來分期。婆羅
門教、佛教、印度教、回教、基督宗教，分別引導過印
度的發展，也分別發展出各具特色的詩歌、寓言、戲劇、
小說作品。曾經通行過的語言如梵文、巴利文、波斯文、
興地文、烏都文，也因多變的聲韻幻化出綺麗豐富的風
情。本書選譯了印度歷史上的代表作，如婆羅門時期：
吠陀經、奧義書；佛教時期：《佛所行讚》、《大莊嚴
經》、《百喻經》；印度教時期：《五卷書》、《四部箴》；
以及近代大文豪：泰戈爾、奈都莎綠琴尼、普雷姜德的
作品。敬邀讀者大眾一同欣賞印度文學多樣的風貌！

印度文學歷代名著選（上）（下）
糜文開　編譯

本書係糜教授繼《印度文學欣賞》的精心編譯，是當今
印度文學的唯一讀本。內容先將印度文學史分成五期敘
述，介紹各期的名著及其作者，於是選錄作品，偏重文
學趣味，上自吠佛讚歌，下迄印度獨立後的國歌及方言
作品，共約四百篇，六十餘萬字。

漂鳥集

泰戈爾　著／糜文開　譯

《漂鳥集》為印度詩哲泰戈爾享譽世界的佳作之一，完成於 1916 年。在這三百餘首短詩中，泰戈爾以清麗抒情的筆調，歌頌大自然的壯闊、體會人生的哲理、抒發對社會的反思、道出對人類的愛，隻字片語中蘊含了無限的哲思與智慧。

曾有位印度醫生說過：「每天讀一句泰戈爾的詩，使我立刻忘卻世上一切苦痛。」的確，泰戈爾《漂鳥集》的文字清新雋永，短短的語句像是捕捉了宇宙萬物的浮光掠影，十分深刻動人。